DECAY STUDIES

DECAY STUDIES

Arthur Seefahrt

SIX GALLERY PRESS

Published by Six Gallery Press 2024

US edition first published in the United States of America in 2024 by Six Gallery Press
P.O. Box 90145, Pittsburgh, PA 15224
www.sixgallerypresspgh.com

ISBN 978-1-989305-20-1

Typeset for Arthur Seefahrt by Donncha Mac Cóil
Cover design by Kelly O'Connor

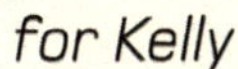

for Kelly

CONTENTS

DECAY STUDIES

*A monk asked Joshu, a Chinese Zen master:
'Has a dog Buddha-nature or not?'
     Joshu answered: 'Mu.' [Mu is the negative
symbol in Chinese, meaning 'No-thing' or 'Nay'.]*

* an excerpt from 'Joshu's Dog', *Writings from the Zen Masters*,
Penguin 2009

THE GREATEST POEM IN ENGLISH

— for WB

another apple
tree

ieldfieldfieldfieldfieldfiel
dfieldfieldfieldfieldfieldfi
eldfieldfieldfieldfieldfield
fieldfieldfieldfieldfieldfie
ldfieldfieldfieldfieldfieldf
ieldfieldfieldfieldfieldfiel
dfieldfieldf eldfieldfieldfi
eldfieldfieldfieldfieldfield
fieldfieldfieldfieldfieldfie
ldfieldfieldfieldfieldfieldf
ieldfieldfieldfieldfieldfiel

THE GARDEN DEMANDS HONESTY

The garden demands honesty
Its contents essential
The apple tree
Its dimensions a constant

Its contents essential
Its agreements direct
Its dimensions a constant
The portal beckoning

Its agreements direct
The shed a temple in ruin
The portal beckoning
Crow seeming as being

The shed a temple in ruin
Fox a tonal sweep
Crow seeming as being
Isolation a fluid

Fox a tonal sweep
Stillness a mode
Isolation a fluid
Light a maneuver

Stillness a mode
Fog opaque
Light a maneuver
Darkness complete

Fog opaque
The apple tree
Darkness complete
The garden demands honesty

THE GARDEN

||||||||||||

It is a thorn
Hard and sharp

When first it gets
Beneath the skin

It does so without sensation

Then like warm sea
A part of you

Pours forth
Is lost always

|||||||||||

The apple tree's clawing branch
Wracked with bulge
Year upon year

Thorny creepers lean
Red fruits swell
Weight opens

A slow wound
A tear in the seam
Of the living wood

Irrevocable this

Later
Pruned and tended
The tree has no way
Of forgetting

||||||||||

It is thirty paces
To the yewed back wall
Of the garden

It is eighteen paces
From one side
To the opposite

The garden's capacity
Does not shift
A perpetual ratio of stone walls

There is the chair
The shed
The apple tree

Sloped eaves beyond
Beyond again sky
Nought else but the garden

Animals visiting the garden
Atomize the garden
Move through isolation like a fluid

Then move into unbeing
Slipping free of
The garden

Yet the garden remains
Immutable dimension
This perpetual being

||||||||

The summer hems us in
Heavy dark leaves
Wet night air

A fox broods
Under the shed

Eyes lit orb-green
By the lantern
Of my cigarette

Between us a hunger
Then it too is gone

The hole only remains
A vacancy staring into night

||||||||

This could be any sky
Cloud reefs lit from below
Black the yew daggers the night

Up from the gaol
Of garden walls and skeletal
Winter apple tree

And at every distance
The sea
The darkening clouds

Headstone rows of nighted houses
I simply cannot see where there is to get to

|||||||

The sun radiates
White indifference
Across the cool dome of uninterrupted sky

A crow passes
Over the garden
Dragging cloudless nothing behind it

June air washes
The garden   The apple tree
Relieving this moment's burden of meaning

What remains
This iridescent blackness of crow riding air
This absence of sky
This absence of moment
This crow only

||||||

I see in the garden
The shed
The apple tree

Bare knuckles
Of reaching branches
Grasping only air

Piled stones becoming walls
From their corners' night stretches inevitable
As songbirds are swallowed into silence

The night devours these objects
Moonless my hand gnawed away black
There is nothing in the garden

|||||

Morning fog
Crocuses pushing from the sodden earth

Waking snails
Calling songbirds to hunt in the grass

The dawn fox
Slips away beyond the sagging shed

Night gives way to day
Trading one opacity for another

All are still cold in this ablative whiteness

||||

Daisies in fresh constellation
Quake a hair's breadth below —

The passage of the blade

III

From its skeleton clawing
The apple tree
Fleshes into its bracts
Slow sapping

The nascent blossom
Waiting to unfurl
Its spoorus illness
Into spring

Spunking window panes
With sick lusting
The urge to continue
To be fruitful

At harvest aglut
Filling a fullness
Who can say
When too much is enough

II

Windfall
Half a sphere
Gone calfskin
Brown and soft

Wasting into the soil
Arboreal life's
Abortive toiling
Feeding the father

Roots clutch and suckle
Pushing slow brown tongues
Over worm-pulped flesh
Saturn licking his fingers after the meal

I

Beyond the apple tree
the shed waits in time
its roof spine sagging
like the gut of a whale

The hands move
doing what hands do
The feet are walking
and sometimes not

Stopping by the wall
the shed is visible
in the garden
It too is hollow

Hailstones hammer the hollow shed
Setting it to sing like a buzzing drum

Sea birds reeve the brining air
Within it spring's raw wet bite

This world is keening a waking song
The frostbitten hand beneath the hot tap

This waking is pain as waking always is
The garden in reality sacrosanct stings

A vessel   nothing more than a vessel
A place one has no concern in being

Which is always in the garden
Which is always in the garden

MIDLANDS

The sky here is pale
white as bone left to
the cold mirror of the sun —
Fields anaemic with winter

No meadows on the land
carved into plots   stone-hemmed
each named and wreathed for
the short holy day

Empty mud roads hash
this land sallow   peppered
with dogless sheep still abroad
when night drops as a sudden bird

A fox on the road
ahead crushed in Xmas
haste displays its splayed skull
colouring the scene

Bogland   the same rich blood-brown
lays bare   inviting
wet and deadly as a lover
long night spent in her embrace

POETRY CANNOT YIELD

The drunkard's sleep
The dreamless void
A sentence without song

Annihilation
which expressionless is love

ABLATION TRIPTYCH II

```
A  shatter  fuhrer
Threat as her fur
Fear as her truth
   shatter  fuhrer
Th e t as her fur
Fe    as her  ruth
   s a te   fuhrer
     e t as her f r
Fe    as  e   r th
      a te  f h er
       t a  he f r
F      a       r th
       a t     h  r
       t    h     r
            r t
       t
```

There is time. There was time. There was a time before the first breath. A forest thrushing with the susurrus of gas exchange. A world scale garden, exosphere grazed by a swollen moon and the nipple of the sea's heaving breast just out of reach. Animals. Then events occur, a man who is a fox approaches an old man and tells him he is and is not a fox, that he has been vexed with this causation, then the old man replies. The next day after the funeral of the fox the old man teaches his student about nothing. The moon swings its lusty urging across the darkened sky, the trees breathe, some after falling, and the old men say nothing. They discuss the soul of a dog

There is time   was time   was a time
before   breath. A forest thrushing
       susurrus of gas exchange. A world s   garden,
          grazed by a swollen moon   nipple
of the sea's heaving breast just out of reach.
Animals.   events occur, a man   is a fox
approaches an old man   tells him he is and is
not a fox,   he has been vexed with this
causation,   the old man replies. The next day
after the funeral   the fox the old man teaches
 is student about nothing.   moon swings its
lusty urging across the darkened sky,   trees
breathe, some after falling,   old men say
nothing.   discuss   the   soul

          time.   was time   was a time
before   breath. A forest
     susurrus of gas exchange A world
               grazed by   swollen moon
          sea   just out of reach
Animals   events   a man   a fox
          an old man   is and is
not a fox   vexed with
causation   the old   replies
     the funeral of the fox
                    nothing   moon swings its
lust   across   dark   sky   trees
breathe   after falling,   old men say
nothing

time.   was   time
before   breath A forest
                                     A world
          grazed by   moon
                                    just
Animals   events   a man   a fox

not
causation the   replies
     the funeral
                          nothing   its
                              dark   sky
                   after falling
nothing

Below us now the dunes unfold for miles as a quilt dropt out of a transcontinental flight seen over the sea falling away from the thrumming porthole window. On the island there is a lighthouse. It rises over the flat sands which slip sparkling into the Atlantic's salted caressing. There are dogs here. Unmanned on the beaches German shepherds roam the flockless shoreline feeding on crab and gifted flight-crew scraps. The strays cobble a life here. When they are not hungry they play, chasing one another into the surf. Then their sleeping legs twitch in their sandy beds as their dreams are hemmed in by the knife blade of the Alps and they do not count the sheep they chase

Below   the dunes unfold   as a quilt
dropt out   over
the sea falling away from the thrumming porthole
window. On the island   a lighthouse
     over the flat sands which slip   into
the Atlantic   There are dogs
     Unmanned on the beaches   shepherds
roam the   shoreline feeding on crab and
               scraps. The strays cobble a
life here. When   not hungry they play,
chasing one another into the surf.   their
sleeping legs twitch in their sandy beds as their
dreams   hemmed in   the knife blade of the Alps
     they do not count the sheep they chase

Below   the dunes unfold
dropt out   over
the sea falling away
            the island   a lighthouse
              flat sands   slip   into
the Atlantic   There are dogs
              on the beach   shepherds
roam the   feeding on crab and
              scraps   cobble
life here When   hungry
chasing one another into the surf
        legs twitch   sandy
dreams are hemmed in   the knife blade   the Alps
      they do not count the sheep they chase

<pre>
                    the dunes unfold
dropt
the   falling
                    island   light
              flat   to
the Atlantic   dogs
                on the beach   shepherds
roam   feed   on
                    scraps
life
          one another   the surf
                twitch
dreams   hemmed in   the knife blade
      they do not count   sheep they chase
</pre>

MU ||||

The sun beams in, futuring angles, glinting into vacant air between the corners of tables and cherry muscle-car-red booth cushions. Another truck rumbles by rattling the roadfacing windows and the sound dies slow. The sole patron feels it after it is beyond hearing, pulsing up the polished chrome counter stool shaft and through the ring on which he rests his feet. There is sizzling. Then there is not, and the heat wafts from the flat cook top mingling with the sunheat building as the afternoon drags on like a limping hitcher. The meal had to have been good, or else the will of the eater. The flavor of salt this far into the desert is the ghost of a sea breeze, pleasant but hurtful

The sun beams   futuring angles, glint   into
vacant air between the corners   tables and cherry
muscle   red booth cushions. Another truck
rumbles   rattling   roadfacing windows   the
sound dies slow. The   patron feels it after it
is beyond   pulsing up   chrome
counter stool   through the ring on which
he rests his feet. There is   Then
there is not   heat wafts   the flat cook
top mingling with   sunheat build   s the
afternoon drags   like a limping hitcher. The
meal had to have been good, or   the will   the
eater   of salt this far into the desert
is the ghost   a sea breeze, pleasant   hurtful

            beams   futuring angles, glint   into
vacant   between   corners   tables
muscle   red   other
rumbles   rattling   roadfacing
        dies slow The   patron   after it
is beyond   pulsing up   chrome
                        through the ring
he   rests   There   is   Then
there is not   heat wafts
     mingling   sunheat build   s the
afternoon   like a limping hitcher
          to have been good, or   the will   the
eater   of salt   is far   the desert
    the ghost   a sea   pleasant   hurtful

vacant   between   corners
muscle   red   other

          dies slow   after
is beyond   pulsing up
                                        the ring
                                    is   Then
            is not

afternoon   a limping
        to have   good   will   the
                        salt   desert
      ghost   a sea

Like a cut underwater the earth bleeds seams of clouds into being. They pulse from the green rupture on the ocean's plane marking from great distance the place of the return. The landing strip is fully equipped with cardboard radar antennae, radio towers all in silent anticipation of a promise made long ago. Messages continue to be received from the pulse of the cloudmaker. The fire rift in the land whispers to its devotees, its thralls, of its monumental indifference. The fire does not react to our dreams. The fire is not aware even that it breaches into the realm of the breathers. It is without sense. Apotheotically continuous it churns in its glaring ring, unaware a cut underwater   earth bleeds seams clouds into being.   pulse from the green rupture   the ocean's plane marking from great distance   place of the return. The landing strip   fully equipped   cardboard radar antennae, radio towers all   silent anticipation   a promise made long ago. Messages continue to be received   the pulse of the cloudmaker. The fire rift   the land whispers to its devotees, its thralls, of its monumental indifference. The fire does not react to   dreams. The fire   not aware   that it breaches   the realm of breathers   without sense. Apotheotically continuous   churns   its glaring ring, unaware

a cut   bleeds
        into being   pulse from the
rupture   marking
distance   place of the return The

radio towers all   silent anticipation   a
promise   continue to be
received   pulse   cloudmaker   fire
rift   whispers   its
thralls   monumental indifference
does not react to   dreams   fire   not aware
        that it
breathe s   Apotheotically
continuous   glaring ring unaware

                                        bleeds

        rupture

                        all   silent
        promise

                                monumental indifference
                                                fire

        breathe s

                                                        unaware

The trees are trees. We can speak of the trees, of how they are trees. Of how they appear to be. Of their trunks' long swilling, of their high thin twigs to remind us they are trees. Of their roots' concealed desperate chasming. We can speak of their living, how they appear to live through growth, through permutation. And you will know what we mean to speak of when we speak of the shifting gaps allowing prisms of light to touch the dark earth sheltering below the canopy, the tops of trees, and the source of the light, and the movement of the light, which is everywhere always, arriving and returning beyond. And do we speak of trees?

trees are trees. We   speak of the trees, of
how they are   Of how they appear to be. Of
their trunks'   swilling, of their high thin
twigs to remind us they are trees. Of their roots'
concealed desperate chasming. We   speak of
their living, how they appear to live through
growth, through permutation. And you   know
what we   speak of when we speak of the
shifting gaps   prisms of light   touch the
dark earth sheltering below the canopy, the tops of
trees   the source of   light   the movement
of   light   everywhere always, arriving
and returning   do we speak of trees?

        trees   speak of   trees
how they   how they appear
their   trunks'   their   high   thin
twigs   remind us they are trees
                                                    speak of
          living   appear to live through
growth   permutation   know
        we   speak
shifting   prisms of light   touch
dark earth   below the canopy
              the source of   light   movement
of   light   everywhere always, arriving
        returning   we speak

                                   speak of   trees
          they are   how they appear
                                             their high thin
twigs   remind us they are trees
                                                      speak of
             living   live through
growth

                                              speak of
                        prisms of light   touch

             the source of   light
                          everywhere always
                                      speak

Bounding the ram runs uphill all ableat and woodily stiff, shallow among the open gorse and weather rounded lichened angles spotting the hilltop where the land is hashed with fences and manifold egging boulders seize the sky as though some unseen thing within were ready to hatch bursting and own it, casting shadow down upon the ragged downy creatures left here to wander dangerless, who have lost the impulse to peer cloudward seeking threat from thinner air — the stratosphere, the wisp making layer of bloodless winds that starshine penetrates always leaking its pale light, too green to see, lavishing us with color somewhere between bone and night, shielding us from our memory of time, which is itself a kind of death

          the ram runs uphill all ableat   woodily
stiff, shallow among   open gorse and weather
rounded lichened angles spotting the hilltop
the land is hashed with fences   manifold egging
boulders seize the sky   some unseen thing
within   ready to hatch bursting
casting shadow down   on   ragged   creatures
left   to wander dangerless, who   lost
                peer cloudward seeking threat from
thinner   air   —   stratosphere   wisp
making layer   bloodless winds   starshine
penetrates always   pale light
            lavishing   with   color   somewhere
between   bone   and   night,   shielding   us
        memory of time, which is   a kind of death

the ram runs uphill   ableat   wood
stiff, shallow among   open gorse
        lichened angles spot   the hilltop
the land   hashed with   manifold
boulders   the sky   some unseen thing
within
casting   down   on   ragged   creatures
left   to wander
            peer cloudward seek   threat
thinner
                    bloodless   winds   starshine
        always   pale light
        lavish   with   color
        bone   night   shielding   us
    memory   which is   a kind of death

                            run   uphill   wood
        stiff   among   gorse
                      lichened
        the land   manifold
                           the sky   some unseen thing
        within

                                                                creatures
                           wander   lost
                                cloudward   seek   threat
        thinner   air
                                                wind   starshine
                      always

                                                color
                                           shield   us
             memory   which is   kind

MU

An old Chinese man told a story about another old Chinese man saying nothing about a dog's soul. In Cape Verde stray dogs roam the beach, their square jaws genetically loyal to a continent which abandoned them. At the counter of the daylit all-night diner a lone unthinking man lifts stray grains of salt with his fingertip, and feels satisfied. And in Micronesia a volcano's cauldron of naked magma roils and glares. In Dublin moonlight licks the dewy lawns and two people slip through a fencebreak around the green to argue about love in the boughs of a fallen tree. And rocking somewhere on a plane or a train the film-maker smiles, then wakes from his dream and looks straight-faced out the window into solid blackness

A   man told a story about another
            man saying nothing about a dog's soul. In
Cape Verde   dogs roam the beach, their
jaws   loyal to a continent which
abandoned them. At the counter of the   all-
night diner a   man lifts stray
grains of salt with his fingertip, and feels
            And in Micronesia a volcano's cauldron
of   magma roils and glares. In Dublin
moonlight licks the   lawns and two people slip
through a fencebreak around the green to argue
about love in the boughs of a   tree. And
rocking   on a plane or a train the film-
maker smiles, then wakes from his dream and looks
                  out the window into   blackness

man told   story
man saying nothing   dog's soul
            dogs roam   beach
jaws   continent
abandoned   counter
      diner   man lifts
         salt   fingertip   feels
                                      cauldron
         magma   roils   glares
moonlight licks   lawns   two people slip
                              green   argue
      love   boughs   tree
rocking   plane   train
maker smiles   wakes   dream   looks
            window   blackness

ABLATION TRIPTYCH III

55

The poems in the MU sequence are page representations
of the text portion of a multimedia installation of the title
DECAY STUDIES. The work was displayed originally at the
Ranelagh Arts Centre, Dublin Ireland in 2018.

Thanks also to the many people without whose critical
support this collection would not be, in particular: Sean
Borodale, Lucie Brock-Broido, Noel Cahill, Matthew
Carey Salyer, Timothy Donnelly, Che Elias, Kevin Finn,
Lizzie Harris, Dorothea Lasky, Julie Kantor, Donncha Mac
Cóil, Meghan Maguire Dahn, Daniel McDonald, Ciarán
Milton, Kelly O'Connor, Beth O'Halloran, John O'Neill,
Jeff Oaks, Liam Powell, Sam Ross, and Daniel Schmidt.